TALES OF FRAME-UPS AND SNORTS

FROM WEBBED THEORIES TO SOPHISTICATED CABALS, "I PREDICTED IT ALL!"

By A.K. SCARLETTE

ask
AIMEE S. KISABOYUN@GMAIL.COM
PUBLISHING HOUSE

TALES OF FRAME-UPS AND SNORTS

By reading this document, the reader agrees that under no circumstances is the author responsible for any losses, direct or indirect, which are incurred as a result of the use of the information contained within this document, including, but not limited to, — errors, omissions, or inaccuracies. For information regarding permission, email the author at kisaboyun@gmail.com.

For information contact:
https://lnk.bio/aimeekisaboyun

Table of Contents

2027, February 6th 5

Chapter 1: 2026 7

2027, February 7th 13

Chapter 2: Together, as One 15

2027, February 19th.. 20

Chapter 3: Test Run 22

2027, March 21st 30

Chapter 4: The Final Ward-ning................................ 32

2027, April 2nd 36

Chapter 5: Ripping off the Mask 38

2027, April 3rd 45

Chapter 6: Maybe, Just Maybe 47

2027, April 14th.. 52

AND A WHOLE LOT OF TOL D-YOU-SO'S! 54

Acknowledgements 55

About The Author 56

2027, February 6

The whole lot of you. You'd think that this bizarre turn of events was unexpected. You're probably sitting at home, reading this, and thinking to yourself that such a memorable date would bring about more joy and probably less pain. Humans would have it figured out by then, I'm sure.

It's not the case. You lucky little creatures, living so obliviously to the pseudo-apocalypse - pseudo because it's not the end of the world (yet, at least), and apocalypse because it just as well might be if we give it a little while longer.

The end of the world. World War Three. What difference does it make? Aren't those terms virtually interchangeable? From where I'm writing this - because writing is the only form of communication, they don't have complete control over these days - I can see the nuclear plumes more common than dead hunks of trees in a forest, sprouting like little mushrooms all over the mountains and valleys of our once-beautiful America.

I'm sure if I was in the Chindoria Federation, there'd be just as many bountiful mushrooms, too - nuclear heralds of what's to come - but I'm nowhere near the battlefront. You may get this letter, and you won't. I must move now, so I'll write more in the following letter.

Much exasperation,
Mark R.

Chapter 1: 2026

I hurriedly stuffed the pen and paper into my backpack, grabbing it from the ground as I retraced my footsteps home, half-expecting to run into an Officer at every corner. I heard the dogs in the distance and knew that they had probably traced my Wi-Fi signal to the location where I sat for hours, writing and watching one of the few accessible television networks left.

Of course, I thought as I tucked my head further into my hooded jacket, trying to stay as inconspicuous as possible. It wasn't like any of these people knew.

If I ever said what I thought, they'd call me crazy. I watched an old lady talking loudly to her neighbor.

"And I tell you, Martha, if they elect Gormond Hakdic again, I won't have it! Absolutely not; he's racist – a bigot, an ableist. He's extremist, Martha!" Cried the old lady, her multiple chins wobbling with the motion of her tiny arms as she gestured grandly about, slung droplets of drool which was no doubt the remainder of her earlier aggression upon a bug sandwich.

That much was evident, and I thought – shifting my gaze quickly as she noticed me watching. She would be a creature of habit, not too removed from her daily rituals to eat anything different and not too wealthy to afford any other foods available at the local store.

"You've never been more right, Glinda. I hear they'll be arresting him soon; serve him right. Can you believe he ran on a campaign of only a 72% tax rate for billionaires? And if Carl Mayarks wins this time, I hear he'd increase the universal basic income all the way from 10,000 to 15,000."

"Exactly," the woman responded one more time to Martha, her eager beady eyes roving to and fro at the thought of more distribution. "Hakdic needs to go. That's all there is to it."

I sighed, shaking my head at these people. They still weren't awake yet. As I turned the corner, I pushed the draped blanket aside and grabbed the power cord lying on the ground, plugging it into my setup.

It wasn't much. I looked around.

My computer, Jerry-rigged like no tomorrow, was my pride and joy. It was on a closed network to prevent any government spies, but I had installed emulators for all types of games and simulations on it. Three monitors were taped to the wall with duct tape, wrapped around the wires and corners to hold them up. My computer itself had almost no casing, with wires spewing everywhere and bizarre coolant fans rigged on the walls of my little hideout as well.

Still, as I plugged my headphones into their port and booted up a few games, it wasn't bad for me.

I am a conspiracy theorist. Everyone around me had labeled me that, at least. My parents were proud supporters of Hakdic, but I was too extreme for even them. Conformity had never been my style, though, so I ended up on the streets, forced to Jerry-rig a computer together and this abandoned "building" – in reality, the patched-up area between two buildings – to live in.

I couldn't get on the internet here, but I still kept up with the worldly happenings through their radio. Believe it or not, they did have some exciting content playing once you realized how infiltrated it had become. Nobody cared that the burger place they ate at had atom-sized trackers placed strategically in the bug meat so toilet companies could track where they shit and sell the information to toilet paper producers. I was the "crazy guy" when I mentioned that.

I was also the crazy guy who, as I listened to the radio station, could pick apart their agenda bit by bit. Never mind that I was at the top of my class, could name every country by memory after looking at a map for thirty seconds, and could beat everyone I used to be friends with in chess.

As soon as I said, "Hey, have you noticed that whenever that radio presenter talks about freedom, he makes sure to slip in a few examples of how freedom has caused tragedies?" I was called a conspiracy theorist.

Figures. I watched my screen flicker as one of the regular power outages coursed through the city. I pulled the paper I had written earlier out of my pocket, lit my oil lantern, and began to read through the information I had collected. It was mainly headlines from news articles.

"Chindoria the latest location of plague outbreak which kills hundreds...Relations between Chindoria and the world become strained as the latest trade regulations create starvation in the lower Federations...Chindoria makes territorial advancements in the economic infrastructure of New India...Nuclear relations..."

Now there was a new one. Chindoria was making the rounds in Their media right now. It was clear that there were some rising tensions between two factions – or that they wanted us to believe that.

But nuclear was new. I scribbled a few notes on my paper and tore off a small chunk. Grabbing a pin, I put the paper up on the wall behind my computer, where my panel of newspaper clippings, notes, and pictures spanned yards.

Nuclear had to be important. It had to be one of the keys – especially because it was mentioned in connection with Chindoria.

And although all the "normal" people were convinced that Chindoria was their mortal enemy, I wasn't convinced.

Chindoria had long since been a scapegoat for almost every issue we had. Bugs? Yeah, that was Chindoria's fault for having too many emissions. Plague? It probably originated from Chindoria, not a lab we'd funded.

Oh, and then there was the economics of the situation. Chindoria was extreme – even though we had such a bizarre economic situation of our own and more debt than we knew what to do with. It was their fault, even though our central economic planning committee was able to set every price known to man and swore up and down they knew what they were doing.

Did they want the bug sandwiches that whatever-her-name was eating daily to cost more? They set it there. Did it backfire? That was Chindoria.

One of my favorite interweb authors had supplied a theory that I was convinced was real. I turned off my computer and lay down on my cot, listening to the noises of the outside world. Something big was coming - a way for Them to take over the world, whoever they were.

Nobody, not even the most significant "Theorists" as we were called by the Collective of Countries and their media charlatans who controlled everything we read and saw and obviously opposed Chindoria, knew who was in control and why they were pulling the strings.

Obviously, they wanted to control, and it was clear that their continued aggressions were only to achieve this goal. The theory went along the lines of claiming that whoever wanted control needed the world to be weak in order to do so. They needed us divided, and why wouldn't they?

Do you think Martha, down the road in all her undiluted glory, would stand a chance against somebody who wanted control? Maybe she would if she had me and other people who actually cared about remaining independent, but she didn't have any support. That was the whole point. She hated her neighbors, they hated her, and they all hated Hakdic, who was, in turn, being paid by the large mono-corporations who backed Carl Mayarks.

I shook my head as I drifted off to sleep. Everyone knew something big was coming - maybe even Martha knew, though she probably didn't know what and was too self-absorbed to understand that it wasn't just about her.

But only us Theorists knew when it was coming and when They were going to take action.

Next year, actually. 2027. And I knew what was coming, just like any other Theorist who had half a brain and could read the headlines.
War was on the horizon.

2027, February 7th

Hey, at least it didn't start in January, right? Yeah, you're probably so relieved that you have an extra month to prepare for the War. You probably realize by now that these letters are - queue the scary music - from the future.

Absolutely shocking. As I'm writing this, I have to wear a hazmat suit - everyone does at this point who's not inside a safe house. I'll let you in on another secret, though. Having to wear hazmat suits doesn't mean you're going to get off work while the War is going on. First of all, they are already manufacturing medications and vaccines for radiation, and even the Hazmat-wearers are having to go to work. You just have to keep your suit on, and you get dirty looks from the already-vaccinated co-workers.

Weird? I'd ask if you were familiar with the crazy divide that medication and having to wear bizarre outfits can cause, but I'm sure you're already dealing with it. The guys who get medicated for radiation get the sublime pleasure of serving their government overlords, and the guys who don't get enslaved or imprisoned. But what's the difference?

Still annoyed,
Mark R.

Chapter 2: Together, as One

I woke suddenly to the blaring sound of alarms. I left my radio on for the white noise while I slept, but something interrupted the broadcast. Rubbing my eyes, I squinted as I tried to listen to the static voice droning over the radio.

"Red alert. War has been declared after nuclear strikes have been sighted and directed from Chindoria. The Collective has issued a wartime decree and will respond without discretion. Countries protected by the Collective..."

I turned it down, cursing to myself. I hurriedly reached into my bag, fishing around for a hazmat suit. Nuclear was no longer the world-ending threat it had once been with the development of new anti-nuclear technologies, but I'd opted for an old-school method.

I could hear alarms blaring in the distance as I bagged up my things, stuffing them into the crate I had tied onto my motorbike.

I couldn't afford to be in a big city if the War had been declared and Chindoria had already launched missiles. Grabbing my phone, I turned it on and sent a single message before turning it back off again.

"Meet me at the ruins in 10."

I sped off, watching lights in all the windows on the dimly-lit street flicker on as normal people suddenly realized that their cozy homes and lives weren't so safe after all. Go figure.

Leaping from my bike, I hurriedly slogged through the mud, the rain continuing to drizzle and the mist growing denser as I made my way into the ruins - where she was waiting.

"Ten minutes, Mark? I barely managed to wake up in ten minutes, and you could have given me a bit longer to get out here." The girl, slightly older than I was, slid out of the shadows. Her piercing dark hair, blue eyes, and smirk told me everything I needed to know.

"You heard the alarms too, then? You didn't have to get up so fast, you know. Just had to put the suit on and go back to sleep."
"You make a good point," she said with a bit of a worried grin. "But I guess it's really happening then? The War has started?"

"And just like we said. Just like we predicted, the entire world is up against Chindoria, and They have already moved to collect every free country, like baseball cards. The only one left is Chindoria, and they're probably already infected if I had to guess."

We both stood in silence for a while, contemplating the fact that our entire world was now at War.

"So, what do we do now? Run about the streets and scream that we told them so? Or do we try actually to do something about it?" She asked finally, turning towards me.

I sighed and ran my hands through my hair. "That'd work if we wanted to be thrown in jail or cloned or worse. But at the same time, people need to know. Maybe we could contact FR.33 and see if we could help him spread the word?"

She raised her eyebrows at me, clearly skeptical. "A good idea, but nobody even knows who he is or how to contact him. I don't think it'd do much good."

"Nobody except for me." Her look went from skeptical to outright baffled, but I continued. "I know I shouldn't have, but you know how I am with hacking - I just have to. And while I was doing it, I found out how to contact FR.33. If you run enough temporal backtraces and find the right data trails, you can get to the source. I have his number."

Her mouth dropped open in awe. "That's brilliant! Okay, yeah, let's call him. Maybe he'll be able to help us somehow."

She pulled out her phone and dialed the number I had held up on a piece of paper. A voice answered just a few seconds after the first ring.

"Hello, who is this?"

We exchanged glances, and I could tell she was as confused as I was.

"Hi. We're looking for FR.33 - please don't hang up, we're Theorists and big fans of your broadcasts, and we need your help. Are you FR.33's wife?"

Silence. Eventually, however, the voice at the end of the line began to speak again. I could tell she was reluctant to speak to us - cautious, probably because They could be listening - but she did speak.

"You'd think that, but no. Just because my logo is of a masked man doesn't mean I have to be married to him. Before I tell you anything else, though, how did you find my number? This is my personal line."

We explained our story and, more importantly, why we were calling. After a few moments of contemplation, she finally replied.

"That does sound like an important cause. I'm tempted to help you, but I'm worried about putting myself and my friends at risk. Nobody knows I'm FR.33 except for you two now, so the only way I can support you is from behind the scenes. So how can we spread the good word that the only reason we're in this damn War is because They want us to be?"

We sat in silence for a little bit, each of us occasionally coming up with an idea or two to try and get the message out. It was challenging to think of a way to get the information out without putting ourselves or anyone else in danger, but eventually, we managed to come up with a plan.

And with FR.33's information and funding, we'd be able to get the word out in no time and hopefully work to end this War before it ended and They had won.

The first thing we had to do was to get it out on the streets - graffiti, posters, leaflets, street art, anything to get the message out. At least, Alice told me, that would be her division. She would be marketing our ideas and trying to help people understand why this War was wrong and what options were out there.

FR.33 would be the funding - operating behind the scenes and helping to get the word out. Through her contacts and money, we'd be able to spread the message in a way that was subtle yet effective.

As for me, well, I had the most enjoyable job of them all. It was time to embarrass some of our oh-so-supreme cosmic and possibly reptile-skinned overlords. That, and find proof to show the world that they were only out for themselves and not the people they were supposed to be protecting.

Interviews would be something I'd be doing.

2027, February 19th

I asked Alice the other day how the progress was going. You won't see any of her progress - and I'm not about to tell you about it either. But hopefully, she's come up with some symbol the smart people can use to tell the other smart people they're smart.

Everyone thinks that smarts are entirely based on IQ. Do a little reading and learn a little psychology. IQ is a bunch of bunk numbers to tell people how much they conform to Big Brother's despises and, in turn, how much Big Brother conforms to their oh-so-gracious overlords. Funnily enough, I think my research is getting close to uncovering who's actually behind this funny thing we call World War Three. If I wasn't so busy dodging bombs and shells, I'm sure I'd have already figured it out.

I'm sure you're living a comfortable, cozy life back before all of this happens. I can promise you that it won't be comfortable in a few years. But like a cute, boiled frog in hot water, you have no idea that you're already uncomfortable. You have no idea that things are already making you feel pain because that pain is only slightly increasing every once and a while. Not a problem, right? Just wait.

Cordially yours,
Mark R.

Chapter 3: Test Run

Interviews are awkward things, but I couldn't spend all day just researching in the dusky dwelling I liked to call home. While Alice was busy trying to stir up Theorists actually to help, I would be trying to find out who exactly was behind all this and also interviewing the bigwigs.

The plan was simple - FR.33 had connections in the media for who knows what reason, and she would be able to get me into some sweet interviews with Them. Maybe not the real high-ups at first, but enough to get us some information and the public's attention.

It was a test run, so I wasn't too worried yet. I'd be able to make it through without issue - at least, that's what I told myself.

The first interview wasn't going to be with one of Them.

"Hello. Glinda, is it? I'm so happy you could join me for an interview for my documentary. Now that the War's started, we're all trying to get a handle on just what's going on. What can you tell us about how you're helping the Collective?"

Her many chins wobbled as the fat lady's lips split into a smile. I shuddered internally but had to remind myself that I had a goal, and I had to stick with it.

"Well, you know I'm so glad Gormond Hakdic has been impeached. He just wasn't as strong-willed as Mayarks is, right? And," she continued, wiping some snot away as it dripped from her nose, "I've been doing some extra factory work now that the War's set in. Anything to help our cause. Besides, we're short-staffed right now."

"Short-staffed?" I leaned back, pretending to be shocked. "You mean the Collective is laying off workers right now. Even in a time of need like this?"

"Well, now, don't you think they know what's best?" I could hear the annoyance in her voice as Glinda's mind began to work overdrive to defend the idiocy of the decision. "They know exactly what's best for us and our country. Hakdic supporters shouldn't be allowed to work in factories unless they've gotten the medicine for nuclear safety. Heaven knows we have people keeling over left and right because of this nuclear stuff, and we can't let it spread."

"Spread, that's right." I nodded slowly and took some notes. "So, it's not just the workers who are affected, but everyone around them who -"

"Yes! And the medicine isn't even that expensive, but it's a necessary precaution." Glinda finished my sentence for me, her chin wobbling as she nodded her head vigorously. "They deserve to be sent off to camps, you know."

"Camps? What kind of camps?" I frowned, curious. Glinda seemed to have forgotten her confusion-induced state and was now talking freely.
"Well, everyone's getting sent off to what they're calling 'safety camps .'And I say send them off, and they should be kept far away and monitored. That way, if anything bad does happen, it's not going to hurt any of us."

The gears in her head were turning, but I wasn't convinced there were any lights on. What was she on about? What had the news been feeding her about nuclear poisoning spreading? I shook my head mentally and banged it against a wall, but I pressed on.

"Interesting. Now, who do you think is really behind this? Is it the Collective, or is it Chindoria?"

"It's definitely not the Collective," Glinda said with a huff. "They're protecting us from Chindoria; we need to be thankful to them. I wish I could thank every one of them that's out there leading the Collective for us every day. They're the real heroes in this War."

"And do you think that Chindoria is behind the War? How would they benefit from this War?" As I asked the question, I could see the cognitive dissonance beginning to come into play as Glinda confusedly stared at me.

"Haven't you heard? Chindoria just wants to take over the Collective and enslave us all! That's why they've been putting all those trade restrictions and why all those diseases are spreading. We need to stand up and fight, or else we'll be conquered by the Chindorians!"

"And -"
I couldn't finish as Glinda was already off on another rant. "Biowarfare," she said, nodding her head without the vaguest idea of what she was talking about. "That's what they're planning to do. We have to be ready for anything."

And with that, the interview was over. I thanked Glinda for her time and assured her that the Collective would keep everyone safe, but I was even more confused than when I had arrived. It might have been just a test run, but I had gotten some information out of Glinda that I was sure would help us in the long run.

Chindoria wanted to take over the collective and enslave us all. Funnily enough, this exact sentiment seemed to be mirrored by everyone already at the whim of the Collective. Fast forward to the war ending, and if they took over Chindoria, they would be hailed as the victors, even though we'd be at the whim and mercy of Their power.

I shuddered at the thought, but it only made me more determined to spread the truth and do what I could to end this War before it was too late. And to do that, I had to do research. I finished loading my camera equipment into the box on the back of my motorbike, donned my hazmat helmet, and headed back to my research cave.

Booting my computer, I dove right into finding out as much about this War and Chindoria as I could. It didn't take me long to find out a few interesting things about the ongoing battle between Chindoria and the Collective, but I did find one thing that stood out.

The guy looked crazy, I'll admit. But since when did Theorists judge people by how they looked? Just because this guy looked like he did daily crack, had a jaw shaped like an elongated banana, hair like the homeless guy you see hanging out by Walmart, and eyes that were so small you could barely see them, he was still a human being.

Ward Zemm was the name of his obviously self-published, self-hosted, and entirely self-constructed video blog. And his videos droned on, but there was one interesting one about Chindoria and the Collective.

"An' I say, an' I say it again, but not a single one o'ya listens to me. Chindoria is a grand ol' conspiracy, an' it's time we all wake up to the reality o' what's really happenin'. Chindoria and the collective are both run by ALIENS, and they're usin' us to get their resources an' keep their secrets. That's why they want the war t' continue. An' if we don't wake up soon, we'll all be livin' in servitude.

"Ya' wanna know why these blue-haired freaks of aliens want the war t' continue? It's cuz they're usin' us as sustenance. They want our resources, they want to be controllin' us, and they can' do that if we work together. And that's why I'm sayin' - wake up an' fight back. We need to stop this War before it's too late."

At the end of his video, Ward left a link to his own website...on the video that was published exclusively on his own website. He was very cheeky, but I appreciated his dedication to advertisement and the art of self-marketing. I quickly clicked on the link (which promptly took me to the same page I had been on), and before I knew it, I was reading more about Ward's theories and the truth behind Chindoria and the Collective.

As crazy as I wanted to believe the guy was - even Theorists have limits - his theories made a lot of sense. Just because his accent was off-the-wall cooky, he was still a thinker and researcher in his own right.

And it didn't take me long to realize just how important Ward's information could be. If it was true - and if he really had proof that some galaxy-traveling aliens had taken over the planet and weren't just pretending to be dolphins like everyone wanted to believe - then we had a chance at stopping this War once and for all.

Despite the fact, indeed, it meant us getting our hands a little dirty.

I pulled open my console and began to type, flying through the code like a surfer on waves - sounds cool, right? Hacking is cool, even though plenty of people don't think so. I wasn't trying to break the law but instead trying to find out more information on Ward's predictions and the truth behind Chindoria and the Collective and also his contact information and where he lived.

Alright! Okay, I admit that I was attempting to break the law a little.

I had always had a knack for hacking, coding, and typing super-fast, but this was different. This was a personal mission - and it wasn't 'just for fun .'As I began to unearth more information, I knew that the Collective wouldn't be happy with me, but someone had to do something. And I was determined to be that someone.

The first order of business was finding Ward.

I scrolled through his website's code, searching for any clue that could point me in his direction. After a few hours of intense searching, I finally found it - a small line of code that listed his address and the content of it all. I'd found it!

I refreshed the page once more to make sure it was a static piece of hidden information...and then realized that I had overlooked the "contact" tab at the top of his site in my excitement. Surely, he hadn't published his address or phone number, I told myself.

My hours spent hacking into his code had been worth it.

One click later, however, I was cursing myself out for having more ADHD than I could handle. Ward had his phone number listed, blinking an alternating red and black, at the top of his contact page. It looked like he had constructed the site in the 1900s, and he probably had.

"In my defense, I didn't know the guy would be so eager to be caught. Stop laughing at me!"

Alice doubled over, tears welling up in her eyes as she listened to my story. "You actually spent hours figuring out nothing. I can't with you!"

"Oh, give it a rest, already. I've got his number now, and it's the result that matters. I'll give him a call in the morning and see if he has any more concrete proof of his alien theory. With any luck, we'll have a real, working theory about who's actually behind this World War by the end of the day."

"Yeah, okay," Alice said as she wiped a tear from her eyes. She was still giggling. "I still think this guy is crazy, but at least I'm not like one of those Anti-Theorists who won't even give him the benefit of the doubt. Hey, at least he's not as crazy as you are. He probably wouldn't have spent hours -"

"Shut up already, Alice!"

2027, March 21st

It's been a while since my last update. You've probably found all these letters all at once, so not for you. But for me, the War has progressed extremely fast in the past month. I've spent all my time researching, running interviews, and trying to find out what's actually going on. I could make more jokes or make fun of the fact that nobody - except for us Theorists - managed to predict this.

But I won't, because of how serious. Bombs exploding in your city level of serious. Alien race is taking over the planet and using us all like super-ultra-enhanced car batteries level of serious. Both of those are actually happening, and this isn't a joke level of seriousness.

I spent my time as a Theorist before this War telling people that they had better watch out for crazy tyrants, the global agenda, and wombats and that we were going to start using a centralized monetary system instead of our much-loved UM currency.

We're being ruled by crazy tyrants, there's a global agenda, mutant wombats have been sighted all over the globe, and we now use a Collective currency. Too bad nobody listened. I guess I have one last shot at this.

Not only friendly terms,
Mark R.

Chapter 4: The Final Ward-ning

I held the phone to my ear. It rang several times before I heard a voice on the other line.

"Ward Zemm, founder of Zemm Truth Network and the Zemm Collective Truth Seeker's Group, how ma' I help ya?"

It was him, all right. Nobody could fake that accent, that's for sure.

"Ward, my name is Mark. I was calling because I'm doing research on Chindoria and the Collective, and I've been hearing some interesting things that you may be able to help me out with."

"Well, now, I'm not sure what sort o' information ya expectin'," he replied. "But, I do know a thing or two about the Collective. Ya want t' hear 'bout it?"

"Specifically, I want to know what proof you have that alien are behind this War and the Collective. I've heard a lot of theories, but nothing concrete."

"The blue hairs is what ya' talkin' 'bout, eh? Well, that's what's behind the wars and the Collective. I've got proof out the butt that these aliens are behind it all. I've seen the blue-haired freaks, and I got a good idea o' what they're doin' with our planet. Sure, they ain't exactly lettin' us in on the secret. They got these little devices sittin' on their heads that make 'em look human, and they ain't talkin'. But, I know what's goin' on, and it ain't good."

"Do you have any videos or documentation that proves your theory?"

"Why sure I do," Ward replied. "Got me a few documents, videos, and other evidence, except I don't. Do you think I'd just be SITTIN' around here broadcastin' these secrets if I had video evidence o' what they' doing? I've seen it with my own eyes, bu' I didn't record it."

I sighed. It was what I was expecting. The guy had no evidence and didn't know what he was talking about. I scribbled down a note next to the page of information I'd collected about him. It read "stinking failure," and it was what I felt like as I moved my hand to close my phone. As I did, however, I heard a guffaw from the voice at the other end of the line.

"Do ya' really think I'd go around talkin' this stuff up if I was a stinkin' failure? There's a reason they haven't caught me yet, I just haven' caught 'em either."

I froze. How did he know what I had just written down? I hurriedly scanned the room, half expecting to see his weird-shaped head and frazzled hair poking out from behind the curtains.

"No need to be scared," he said with a chuckle. "I just got me a few eyes on ya', that's all. And by eyes, I mean ya' computer. You're smart, kid, but you need more security measures if you want to avoid being tracked. But, I ain't here to lecture ya' on that. I'm here to offer ya' a deal."

"What kind of deal?" I asked cautiously.

"I'm willing to give ya' access to the evidence I have if you'll find more. I can see all ya' cute little notes, and I think I have a general idea of what ya' trying to do. If ya' interested, I can get ya' into a few places where you can start lookin'. Your cute little interview gig should be enough to get the hat off the cat, though I don't think that's the sayin'.

"If you'll go and interview one of these blue-haired buzzards on live TV, all you should have to do is pull off their hat, and the hologram disguise will be gone. Then, you'll have yourself a real live alien to interrogate, and I'll provide ya' with the evidence I've gathered so far. Deal?"

My mind raced as I thought about his offer. It was a lot to take in, but it could work. I knew that if I got one of these aliens on live

TV, people would be more willing to believe what we were saying and maybe even join us in our cause.

FR.33 had already mentioned she was going to try to get me some interviews on live TV, so this could be the way to make it happen.

I took a deep breath and nodded my head. Ward laughed.

"I see ya took to the idea that I hijacked your computer. Ya' got yourself a deal, kid. You contact FR.33 and get yourself an interview with Gary Iceberg. I've already loaded the information you need on ya' computer."

Click. He hung up, but I had already heard enough.

I looked at my computer and saw the documents he'd given me. It was as if he'd read my mind - everything I needed was here. It was fascinating - he had drawings of the supposed blue aliens that were running Chindoria and the Collective, he had accounts of information being stolen, and he even had evidence of alien technology.

I quickly sent FR.33 a secure message with my request for interviews and crossed my fingers that she would come through for me.

"Interview confirmed. Going to take place on April 2nd. Will send details on the location."

2027, April 2nd

Oh boy. You think you're nervously waiting for the world to inevitably fall face-first into War, and you just wait until you have to interview an evil galactic alien capable of taking over the entire human race through manipulation like I'm about to.

That's the actual definition of nervous. I can't even handle thinking about it. I'm going to have to interview, expose, and escape from one of the most evil sentient beings on this little space rock we call home. It really puts things into perspective.

People always say to listen to your parents. What they forget to mention is that if your parents are listening to your government, you probably shouldn't listen to them. It's like a human centipede of collectivist thinking being fed from one party to another till it reaches your toddler-like ears and digs into your skin like a fungus, infecting every free thought you have until you regurgitate it and use it to build a mosh-pit of your own brainwashed ideas.

Please don't listen to anyone unless they're right. It's time for you to pull the mask off of any of the weird, false ideas that you're having - like maybe you think politicians have your best interests at heart, or maybe you think those jeans make you look slim. I don't know you, but I doubt they do. And while you work on that, I'm going to go expose one of these blue-haired alien freaks to the entire world to save the world from the world.

Not looking forward to this,
Mark R.

Chapter 5: Ripping off the Mask

I sat nervously. I could feel the sweat pouring over my face as I waited for Gary Iceberg, the CEO of Megahard Computers - and an obvious alien if there ever was one. He was basically in the tech industry at this point. He owned three out of the four social media that hadn't been banned for being from Chindoria, and he had a lot of power and influence in the tech world.

I was here to figure out what he was really up to and hopefully get some evidence on tape that could show the world the truth behind Chindoria. It wasn't going to be easy - these aliens had been at this game for centuries and knew how to keep their secrets.

Just then, the door opened, and in walked Gary Iceberg. He looked as ugly as usual. He had doggy-like features, tons of scarves and wraps, and an air of superiority about him. He eyed me like a cobra as he walked over to the chair opposite of me and sat down.

He leaned back and smiled. "So, Mark - what are we talking about today?" he said in a manner that was only too clearly practiced and glib.

I didn't waste any time. "And. We. Are. Live. I'm here with Gary Iceberg, CEO of Megahard Computers. We're here today to talk about your recent honorable contributions to the Collective and the war efforts against Chindoria."

He smiled. "So, I take it you heard about my generous donations? Well, that's not something I want people to know about. I donated to the Collective because my son is fighting bravely at the front, and I love this country. I want to see it win this War."

I nodded my head, but I couldn't help but recoil from the obviously practiced manner in which he spits out these words. I had to get to the bottom of this.

"Yes, you've been very generous in your donations, but let's talk about why you're really here. What is it you're really trying to accomplish by helping the Collective?"

He leaned forward and smiled. "Chindoria is a menace to this world and must be stopped. I want to help the Collective in any way I can, even if it means risking my own safety."

Here it was. Here was a way to get him uncomfortable. "I see, so would you say that the people of this nation deserve the nation to themselves? That's basically why you're trying to stop Chindoria, right?"

He hesitated for a moment before responding. His face grew serious, and he seemed to think intently on the matter. "Absolutely. It's not about me or you. It's about these people and their heritage of freedom and independence."

I had him. I reached for my bag and grabbed the piece of paper I had tagged with the red tape. Holding it up so the camera could see, I hit him with one of the heavier questions.

"That seems to contradict your latest business decisions. I have a document here that shows your latest land purchases which just so happen to coincide with your latest court cases. From what this says, you've been purchasing up land throughout the country by illegally draft-canceling smaller landowners and then reselling it to Ultr International, which now controls 81% of all land within the country. Doesn't that seem like a blatant contradiction to what -"

"I don't see how that's relevant," his face was red, his teeth clenched, and his eyes wide with rage. He still smiled, but I could see his anger boiling over. "That's a highly offensive question to ask me, considering how my contributions to the Collective haven't been recognized. Now, if you'll excuse me, I think it's time for me to go."

He stood up abruptly, but I knew better than to let him head for the door. There was one last part of the interview that I needed to catch on camera.

I lunged toward him, grabbing for the top of his head and his hair, and yanked off the hairpiece. It came away easily in my hands as he screamed in pain. There it was - the ugly truth about him revealed at last.

Gary Iceberg sat there, his bald and glistening dome exposed in the camera's light. He didn't change into a blue alien. He was just bald.

"I-I'm so sorry," I stammered. "I didn't mean to..."

My voice trailed off as I watched him. His face wasn't contorted into anger at my lunge. It was fear. The color drained from his face as he quickly felt the top of his head, and relief rushed over him as he turned toward me.

"What? How dare you assault me. Guards! Security!"

But I knew what he had been looking for. I lunged toward him again, desperately scraping at his shining dome as I felt something give way. Bzzt. I heard the sound of electricity as something inside him shut down, and I pulled away a metal device from his scalp.

With a flicker and a shock, Gary Iceberg was no more. In his place sat a blueish, alien-like creature with a trembling, emotionless face. He looked from me to the camera, then back again.

His hair was blue, his body a blueish-gray. Its eyes were wide and black, almost exactly as if they were made of glass. Its mouth was small, and it had no teeth.

Even in this form, though, I could see the rage spreading through the creature's body. "How DARE you," he growled, his voice robotic and hollow.

I stepped back, my heart pounding in my chest. I glanced around desperately and saw the guards running into the room.

"They'll cut off the broadcast for me, you know. You haven't won! You haven't. Security, execute this man!"

I cursed under my breath. Why did it have to come to Alice's horrible plan? With one swift motion, I grabbed the camera and leaped from the window, my arms flailing as I tried to hold onto the camera. As I hit the roof of the shabbily constructed landing area, I heard the glass shatter behind Gary Iceberg and me screaming in rage.

It was over. I had done it. I had ripped off the mask and exposed the real face behind Chindoria's lies. Now, it was up to the world to decide what to do - provided they even saw the live broadcast. I tumbled through the building, turning down each path I had carefully memorized in the days before the interview.

"Left, right, left - no right, right again, left, and right? What was Alice thinking? Center, that's it!" I muttered to myself as I rounded the final corner and spotted a familiar figure in the dark alley.

"Get on the bike!" Alice shouted, and within seconds I had my hands wrapped tightly around her waist as we flew away from the scene.

I had the recording safe and secure on the camera, and hopefully, the live TV broadcast had actually gone through due to FR.33's meddling.

"So, how did it go?" Alice yelled back to me over the wind. "Did you get it?"

I nodded. "I got it. I had a moment of doubt because I thought he was just bald - it turns out he wasn't bald, just blue and alien!"

Alice sighed. "That's a relief. We can finally back up what we've been saying all along and hopefully get those lying aliens out of our skies for good. I still can't believe THIS was the big thing we've been warning everyone about."

"They're more dangerous than you'd think! Do you think Megahard Computers hasn't killed countless landowners in order to expand their empire?"

Alice shook her head. "You're right. Still, blue alien or not, we have the evidence now, and that's all that matters. Let's get back and show everyone what we've got. We'll finally be able to meet up with FR.33, too."

Suddenly, however, flashing red lights announced the arrival of police cars. On each side of my motorbike, sirens began to blare, and patrol cars began to speed toward us. We were surrounded.

Alice cursed and quickly veered off the main road, driving into an alley and taking every twist and turn she could find. My heart was pounding in my chest, but I tried to stay as calm as possible.

This was it - the moment of truth. If we got away, then all our hard work would have been worth it.

Finally, after a few more death-defying maneuvers, Alice managed to get us away from the police, and we were back on the main road. Now came the hard part. High-speed chase? Easy.

Convincing a bunch of sheep that the shepherd was planning to eat them? Not so easy. Not easy at all.

2027, April 3rd

It's going live. Our broadcast revealing my "success" - of finding a blue alien freak and tearing his wig off, literally - didn't do so well on live TV. Even with the help of my highly ingenious network, they still managed to pull it off of the web with reasonably little effort. That being said, we're not exactly behind on our schedule.

We never expected it to really make a wave with the broadcast. Now, it's time to edit up all the information and turn it into something that we can actually advertise. Maybe you'd like to see the broadcast too? I'll include a recording of it, encoded into my writing. Now you just need the passcode to watch it. Wouldn't you like to know what it is?

Going to keep this brief as we're swamped fending off the blue aliens from stealing our recording of one of Their member's heads.

I expect some of my letters will get lost in the transition back in time, so I'll make sure to give a brief recap here and in all further messages. The end of the world is predicted. The end of the world happens (we told you so). Research initiated. Blue aliens found. Plot revealed.

Hoping for tomorrow,
Mark R.

Chapter 6: Maybe, Just Maybe

We arrived at the specified meeting location with FR.33 around three hours earlier. As I got off the bike, though, I nearly jumped out of my pants as a figure emerged from the rocky landscape we had pinpointed in our earlier communications.

"Well, ya' really managed ta' get the evidence. I didn' think you'd do it, but I can't complain.",

I recognized that bizarre accent anywhere. Ward stood in front of me, his homeless-looking face only accentuated by his wardrobe. A bathrobe draped over his boney figure, a full leather belt slung around his waist, crocs on his feet, and a black hat covering his face.

"You cut it close, kid," Ward said with a smirk. "We're gonna need to move fast if we want to get this broadcast out in time. Heard the news yet?"

"What news?"

"They announced it hours befor' ya interview. Guess maybe one of the higher-ups guessed that something was wrong. There's a final D-Day effort being launched against the Chindorian front in just a few hours. We need this broadcast to go everywhere, or everyone is goin' ta die."

"He's not wrong," a voice said behind us. I turned around to see a woman standing there, her ebony skin clashing with a beautiful white dress. She wore business attire, large earrings, and an air of confidence.

"FR.33?" I asked in disbelief, and the woman nodded.

"Yes, I am," she said with a smile. "You've done a remarkable job here tonight. Now let's get to work on making sure the rest of the world hears your message."

The next several hours were a blur as FR.33 got to work on making sure our broadcast went out everywhere it needed to go. The news was spreading like wildfire, and people began to take notice of what we had uncovered about the Collective and Chindoria - their lies, their misdeeds, and their hidden agenda for humanity. We didn't have them admitting on camera what they were trying to do - we just had all the statistics, evidence, and proof for that.

What we did have, though, and what was arguably the most effective, was live proof that there was a literal blue alien controlling Megahard Computer - and everyone knew Megahard Computers worked very closely with the Collective. We had exposed the enemy to its fullest, and now it was up to the rest of the world to react.

FR.33 made sure to edit the video in a way that it contained undeniable proof of Their agenda and was impossible to refute. Now it was just a waiting game. All we could do now was sit back and watch the world react - and hope they would do the right thing.

"Think they'll actually wake up? I mean, there's so much evidence here, but will it be enough to make a difference?" Alice said, her voice echoing one of my key concerns.

"It's hard to know. We don't have much data from the front lines, where the D-Day effort should be taking place right about now. If our evidence got out in time, you might even see mass defects from the army..." FR.33's voice trailed off.

"Why don't we check?" I responded, my hands already reaching for the computer keyboard. We were all connected to the same server, and within minutes I had hacked into the live field reports.

It didn't take much coercing of Their system either. Apparently, even blue aliens use "password01" as their password on some very critical documents. Who knew?

As the reports began to fill the screen, I smiled. The news was good - excellent. "See here?" I pointed toward some jumbled numbers on the screen. It doesn't look like much, but these are casualty numbers; these are some other statistics...how many people are eating bug sandwiches, for example...and HERE are the numbers of defects. If we correlate this with previous numbers, which they've actually published -"

"It's up over nearly 3,000 percent," Alice said, her voice filled with relief.

"It's not nuf' to stop the alien invasion or the War," Ward said as he chewed on a packet of gum - which, from the looks of him, had been his first meal in weeks, "but at least it shows what'll happen if they know the truth. Just takes one to wake up, and one life is saved."

I ate a sandwich I had packed earlier as I sat on my cot back at my hidey-hole. It wasn't much, but it was home. It also wasn't a bug sandwich, which was more than all those sheep could say.

I heard a rustling of fabric, and a hand pushed my blanket covering aside. I started to get up but sat back down as I realized it was Alice.

"I figured you'd still be up," she said, smiling.

I nodded and smiled back. "Yeah, I couldn't sleep for some reason - my mind is racing. It's like, we managed to do it. But is that enough? Will they actually change things?"

Alice shrugged. "Who knows? All we can do is hope. We did our part and exposed what we knew. I guess now we need to find more evidence and release more."

"Yeah, that and avoid being caught. I have a feeling that They're looking for us right now. And heck, we didn't even expose any bigwigs except for that blue chump in charge of Megahard Computers."

Alice sat down beside me, and I put my arm around her. I'd known Alice for a long time, and I knew she had her own secrets. I had always wanted to ask her how she managed to get involved with all of this, but now didn't seem like the right time.

Instead, we just looked out at the night sky - thinking about what else we could do and what the future would bring.

We had a long road ahead of us, but - as corny as it sounds - the truth sets you free. That sounded really corny, but I'd always been a sucker for corny things.

2027, April 14th

Wow, I bet you're wondering where I've been. Haha. Time travel joke, you're getting all of these letters at the same time. I've been good. The hunt for us and for "misinformation" - which is what they're calling anything we Theorists put out - has essentially tripled in a few days.

That's what they do when we get close to the truth. They hunt us down, say we're the ones who are crazy, and claim we're dangerous extremists. The whole nine yards. It's a crazy situation, but there's one thing that tends to remain steadfast. The guys who want to ban information are usually the bad guys.

Actually, there's never been a case in history where the people cracking down on fundamental human rights turn out to actually want what's best for you. At best, they just convinced you that they were good when in fact, they just won. But they're not going to win this time.

There are too many people willing to fight for what's actually right, willing to wake up. I saw Glinda this morning on my usual walk to the ruins. She's one of those "sheep" who enjoys being slaughtered, I think. Or she used to be. I overheard her talking about blue aliens. From what she says, she "always knew all along that there was something fishy about Megahard Computers and that psycho CEO," and she's more than happy to stick to that story.

It's better than nothing, right?
Feeling motivated,
Mark R.

AND A WHOLE LOT OF TOL D-YOU-SO'S!

Acknowledgements

' All images: Flaticon.com'. The page arts have been designed using images from Flaticon.com

Galaxy designed by Freepik from Flaticon

Invasion designed by Freepik from Flaticon

UFO designed by Freepik from Flaticon

UFO designed by Freepik from Flaticon

Alien designed by Freepik from Flaticon

Alien designed by Freepik from Flaticon

Gas mask designed by Freepik from Flaticon

Face mask designed by Freepik from Flaticon

Explosion designed by Freepik from Flaticon

Shells designed by Freepik from Flaticon

Destroyed designed by Freepik from Flaticon

Soldier designed by Freepik from Flaticon

Destruction designed by Freepik from Flaticon

Nuclear-weapon designed by Freepik from Flaticon

About The Author

Accidental author Aimee Kisaboyun holds a Forensic Medicine Cert., Cert. in Early Childhood Education & Care Competency and a Diploma in Counselling.

She is also a Paediatric Hypnosis Coach, Parents Coach, Kids Coach, ICF Accredited Life Coach, and Speaker and works around crime-fighting heroes. Despite her struggles to read and not having the ambition to write as a child, in 2020 she shared her story in a Multi-Author Best-selling book and it changed her life and business.

That she has many strings to her bow is no surprise to anybody who knows her, as she is a serial entrepreneur. She describes her mind as very active and uses writing to get her ideas out and focus her thoughts. Her inspirations come from far and wide. She looks to world events, real-life stories, and personal experiences.

Through her writing, she hopes to impress on her readers that whatever life throws at you, there is always a funny side.